Harry Guthrie-Smith

Crispus

A Drama

Harry Guthrie-Smith

Crispus
A Drama

ISBN/EAN: 9783337303242

Printed in Europe, USA, Canada, Australia, Japan

Cover: Foto ©Andreas Hilbeck / pixelio.de

More available books at **www.hansebooks.com**

CRISPUS

A DRAMA

BY

H. GUTHRIE-SMITH

WILLIAM BLACKWOOD AND SONS
EDINBURGH AND LONDON
MDCCCXCI

TO

MR HERBERT SPENCER

𝕿𝖍𝖎𝖘 𝕯𝖗𝖆𝖒𝖆 𝖎𝖘 𝖉𝖊𝖉𝖎𝖈𝖆𝖙𝖊𝖉;

FOR,

WHILE THE MERE MENTION OF THE

NAME OF THE AUTHOR OF 'THE PRINCIPLES OF PSYCHOLOGY'

TENDS TO MAKE ITS IMPERFECTIONS MORE MANIFEST,

THERE IS PLEASURE IN THE ACKNOWLEDGMENT

OF INTELLECTUAL OBLIGATION.

CRISPUS.

THE story of Crispus is well told in Gibbon's
'Decline and Fall of the Roman Empire,' and
what follows here is, in the main, his account of
that unfortunate prince.

Crispus, the eldest son of Constantine by his
first wife Minervina, and the heir-presumptive of
the empire, was invested with the title of Cæsar
and the administration of the Gallic provinces,
where the inroads of the Germans gave him an
early occasion of signalising his military prowess.

In the civil war which broke out soon after-
wards, the father and son divided their powers.
The siege of Byzantium, held by the Emperor
of the East, Licinius, was attended with great
labour and difficulty. The naval commanders of
Constantine were summoned to his camp, and

received his positive orders to force the passage
of the Hellespont.   Crispus was intrusted with
the execution of this daring enterprise, which he
performed with so much courage and success, that
he deserved the esteem and excited the jealousy
of his father.   This naval victory determined the
event of the war, and the names of Constantine
and Crispus were united in the joyful acclamations
of their subjects, who loudly proclaimed that the
world had been subdued, and was now governed
by an Emperor adorned with every virtue, and by
his illustrious son, a prince beloved of heaven,
and the lively image of his father's perfections.
The public favour, which seldom accompanies old
age, diffused its lustre over the youth of Crispus.
He deserved the esteem and he engaged the affections of the court, the army, and the people.   This
dangerous popularity soon excited the attention
of Constantine, who, both as a father and a king,
was impatient of an equal.   Instead of attempt-
ing to secure the allegiance of his son by the generous ties of confidence and gratitude, he resolved
to prevent the mischiefs which might be apprehended from dissatisfied ambition.   An edict of
Constantine, published about this time, manifestly

indicates his suspicions that a secret conspiracy had been formed against his person and government. By all the allurements of honours and rewards, he invites informers of every degree to accuse, without exception, his magistrates or ministers, his friends, or his most intimate favourites,—protesting with a solemn asseveration that he himself will listen to the charge, that he himself will revenge his injuries. The informers, who complied with so liberal an invitation, were sufficiently versed in the arts of courts to select Crispus, his friends and adherents, as the guilty persons. The time had now arrived for celebrating the august ceremony of the twentieth year of the reign of Constantine, and the Emperor for that purpose removed his court from Nicomedia to Rome, where the most splendid preparations had been made for his reception. Every eye and every tongue affected to express their sense of the general happiness.

In the midst of the festival the unfortunate Crispus was apprehended, by order of the Emperor, who laid aside the tenderness of the father without assuming the equity of a judge. The examination was short and private, and as it was

thought decent to conceal the fate of the young
prince from the eyes of the Roman people, he was
put to death either by the hand of the executioner
or by the more gentle operation of poison. The
innocence of Crispus was universally acknow-
ledged, and as soon as the afflicted father dis-
covered the falsehood of the accusation by which
his credulity had been so fatally misled, he published to the world his repentance and remorse,—
he mourned forty days, during which he abstained
from all the ordinary comforts of life, and for the
lasting instruction of posterity he erected a golden
statue of Crispus, with this memorable inscrip-
tion—

"TO MY SON, WHOM I UNJUSTLY CONDEMNED."

H. G.-S.

Mugdock Castle,
Strathblane, 16th April 1891.

PERSONS REPRESENTED.

CONSTANTINE, the Emperor.

CRISPUS, his son.

LACANTIUS, formerly tutor to Crispus.

PROCOPIUS,
ARBACUS, } friends to Crispus.
DION,

NEPOS.

VILERNUS.

AURELIUS, servant to Vilernus.

METUS,
CYRUS,
ATTALUS, } officers to Crispus.
DECIUS,

GRIPPA, page to the Empress.

FAUSTA, the Empress.

HELENA.

Citizens, Soldiers, Prisoners, Officers, Courtiers, Admirals, Guards, Heralds, Ladies.

Scene—SOMETIMES IN BYZANTIUM—SOMETIMES IN NICOMEDIA—SOMETIMES IN ROME.

CRISPUS.

ACT FIRST.

SCENE I.

Byzantium.   Antechamber to the apartments of FAUSTA.

Enter LADIES *and a* PAGE.

1*st* LADY.

Run quickly, Grippa, to the camp for news.

GRIPPA.

Madam, I go.

2*d* LADY.

Oh stop !   About the war.

A

GRIPPA.

About the war.

1*st* LADY.

Also the Prince's health.

2*d* LADY.

Prince Crispus' health ; do not forget.

1*st* LADY.

Nor this,

That instantly Vilernus must attend
The Empress Fausta.

GRIPPA.

Ladies, I shall bring
Both eunuch, and the latest news from camp.

[*Exit* PAGE.

2*d* LADY.

How has our Royal Mistress passed the night ?

1*st* LADY.

In watchful wakefulness, or when she sleeps—
Sleep a misnomer for her broken dreams—
Her tongue still runs on battles, wrecks, and
    deaths.

Alas! there is no wonder that her dreams,
Reflecting sad realities, should dwell
On the most bloody scenes that now occur
So near her couch; yet the Physicians Royal
Declare her present malady is born
Of anxious mind; for ever since the war
Outbrake between Licinius, traitor he,
And our great Emperor, mighty Constantine,
She has been much perturbed, and even more
Since 'twas determined that the warlike Prince—
That very day returned from foreign strife,
With scarcely time to greet his bosom friends—
By order of his sire the Emperor,
Should meet the greater navies of the foe,
And drive them from the Straits.   Her fears, I
        think,
Are for Prince Crispus' life; for when in talk
I merely hinted of an evil chance,
At once she bade me silence angrily :
Said, "Do you wish it so, that thus your thoughts
Speak out?"   Ha! Grippa has returned.

                              [*Enter* PAGE.

                    2*d* LADY.

                                    What news?

1*st* LADY.

Any fresh messenger in camp? Speak! speak!

2*d* LADY.

How goes the war?

1*st* LADY.

Is the Prince Crispus safe?

2*d* LADY.

He is not slain? Is't victory, or defeat?

PAGE.

I cannot tell; but here——

1*st* LADY.

The eunuch comes.
[*Enter* VILERNUS.
The latest news, Vilernus, from the fleets?

VILERNUS.

It has for hours been stale. Last night the fleets,
After an even battle, waged all day,
To their respective harbours each withdrew.

1*st* LADY.

That still the latest news?

2*d* LADY.

Nought fresh?

VILERNUS.

Nought fresh.
These are the latest tidings.   I was bade
Attend the pleasure of her Majesty.

1*st* LADY.

She now is stirring, and will presently .
Speak with you even here; till then she bids
That you should wait for her.

VILERNUS.

It shall be done;
Her Majesty's commands shall be my care.
[*Exeunt* LADIES *and* PAGE.
Wait! and for one who construes every breeze,
Ay, every breath, a gale; ever suspects
That every whisper tells her secret thoughts;
Whose slightest ailment seems the touch of Death.

Wait!   They shall wait on me who deem my mind
Emasculate—a woman's!
Already does the Emperor suspect
Crispus of treachery, and fraud designed.
Constantius, Fausta's son, must fill his place—
A child in years, weak by inheritance.
'Tis but for me to push thought into act.
In this the Empress shall share sin with me;
For I have made her credit that her son's
Rights, person, are in danger, as they are,
From Minervina's son; and secrets shared
Solder participants.   By this, and through
Her vacillating humours, I shall gain
Riches, respect, and deference from men;
Shall wear the silks of life, and on decease
Of the great Constantine—his children then
Being in leading-strings—shall sway a throne.
Am I a villain thus to tongue my thoughts?
A villain! shall such name be given me
Because I pleasure can assimilate
From other acts than those termed virtuous?
Himself save from himself, how shall a man
Correct, how patch himself with clay, except
He himself gather it?   For men are born
Evil or good, with such potential stays

Or drags as form the finished character.
Nor these extraneous, but in self contained ;
Not to be therefore blamed or praised are parts,
But used.
Pleasure's the key to life, howe'er possessed,
And howsoever won.
This being so, infraction of the best
May be nefarious ; yet to each man
There's one and only one criterion.
Who feel remorse have sinned against themselves.
There is no personal sin where no remorse
Is felt, and that I ne'er have known, nor shall—
I who seek rather practice for myself
Than abstract ethics, save for mine excuse.
I am forbidden offspring to prolong
My life ; and but a dreamer's fantasy
Is life to come, therefore I am resolved
To treat the present as the whole, and drain
From it all good ; by this my state shall thrive.
And now to shape the steps.

Enter FAUSTA, HELENA, *and* LADIES.

FAUSTA.
No news from sea ?

VILERNUS.

Empress, no more than that our fleet set sail
At early morn.

FAUSTA.

Whence blows the wind?

VILERNUS.

The wind
All day has blown due south.

FAUSTA.

Is't so, indeed?
The Lady Helen says——

HELENA.

A prophecy,
To be fulfilled!

VILERNUS.

What prophecy is this?

FAUSTA.

This lady says that in the war now waged
Between Prince Crispus and the admirals,
The south wind favoured him, helping him stem

The northern flowing Hellespont.   He sailed
At dawn ; by now the victory's complete.

VILERNUS.

The south wind favoured him, so much we know;
Likewise 'tis true he sailed at dawn, but how
The lady knows of victory so soon,
Seeing no messengers have yet arrived,
I cannot guess.

HELENA.

But I—I know it well.

VILERNUS.

And wherefore, Lady, are you so assured ?

HELENA.

Because I am a woman, and our sex
Can trip the airy ladder of deduction
With nimblest feet.
And thus, while men flounder from fact to fact,
Creeping inductively, we scale the heights
And bring down certain truths ; but oftentimes,
At the elevation giddy, lose our marks,
And cannot verify the road to those
Who question of each stage, tho' not the less

Those stages known to us. I tell the truth.
Because of victory, the news comes slow,
For our men still pursue, nor can be spared
A single mariner—the gods be praised !—
To tell of victory, glorious and complete.

VILERNUS.

Complete ?

HELENA.

          The same, there is no mediate way
Against such odds. The western armament
Tallies, in all, but seven score trieremes,
Whilst the commanders of Licinius
Three times outnumber us, with craft late skimmed
From seas still by that rebel traitor swayed.

FAUSTA.

It may be so : but, ladies, now retire,
We would have private speech.

HELENA.

                    Empress, we go.
                    [*Exeunt* LADIES.

FAUSTA.

Vilernus, we desire your thoughts, your speech.

VILERNUS.

What can your servant do?

FAUSTA.

Rather undo!
'Tis a most cursed wrong that we intend
This son of Constantine, and I could swear
This girl, no matter how, has guessed the truth,
For Lady Helen loves the Prince, and love
Can see where hate is blind.

VILERNUS.

It cannot be.
The disproportion of the fleets is known.
Hope, rather than assurance, even friends
Hold of his cause, and on authority
Of truth, the losses of the fleets last night
Were equal in the war.   Shall Crispus, then,
With weakened forces hold again his own?
For every vessel lost to him will prove
More of a loss than to the enemy
That vessel counted thrice.   It cannot be
But that the Prince's fleet shall be engulfed
In Hellespont, and that the stepson thus,
Whom you so hate, shall be removed, and grasp

No more your Royal son's inheritance.
Should he be slain——

FAUSTA.

Heaven grant otherwise !

VILERNUS.

Then should disgrace attend his arms, for one
Must happen of the two, the Emperor
Awaits convenient opportunity
To pluck him from his present eminence.

FAUSTA.

Defeat at hands of foe is not our work.
What has been said we now reiterate,
That to his hurt we will not stir a foot.
Hark ! hark ! a steed hard pushed,——

VILERNUS.

And one whose pace
Prefaces weighty news.

FAUSTA.

Oh pregnant hour !

VILERNUS.

Ay, now our fate's in birth!

[*Enter* AURELIUS.

FAUSTA.

Your news? Your news?

AURELIUS.

The written tidings for the Emperor——

FAUSTA.

Fellow, be brief.

AURELIUS.

Have been detained in camp.
But to be brief—Prince Crispus' victory
Is full, great, glorious.

FAUSTA.

And he himself?

Alas! not dead?

AURELIUS.

The Prince has not been hurt.

FAUSTA [*aside*].

My son's inheritance!

VILERNUS.

Unfold your tale.

AURELIUS.

Shortly, the hostile admirals have fled,
Their mariners slain, taken, or dispersed,
And of their greatest vessels eight score sunk.
These joyful tidings cheer the astonished camp.

VILERNUS.

Ha! this is news indeed; you may retire.
Yet stay, how did the men in camp behave
Hearing this happy news?

AURELIUS.

Tumultuous joy
Had eased strict discipline.

VILERNUS.

Aurelius,
Do not depart, but wait our charge without.
[*Exit* AURELIUS.

FAUSTA.

Are these the great results of all your plans?
The stars look black to us, I shall be warned.

VILERNUS.

Stars! Let them wink at man's infirmities.
Not so. The prestige of the warlike Prince
Would have been dimmed, but for a period
Too short in likelihood for our desires.
His very fortune now shall prove his foe.
Old plans have failed, 'tis true, yet in their fall
Shall Crispus be undone ; for Constantine,
Jealous of single rule and precedence,
Lusts after empire, life in the ears of men,
Ambition and its adnate attributes.
Now from this present action shall his son
From youthfulness, also because to war
On seas is strange to Roman arms, eclipse
His shadowed sire.
Already—'tis the malady of thrones—
The Emperor dreams of plots, conspiracies,
Cabals, and insurrections 'gainst his throne.
To whom will likelihood more surely point
Than to his heir as gainer by such acts?
I shall incite——

FAUSTA.

No more !

VILERNUS.

Empress, beware !
The Prince has thwarted by this victory
Our former plans : fail not to recollect
That by our present action we decide
Your own son's fate.

FAUSTA.

I fear Lacantius.

VILERNUS.

Lady, fear nought.   As in distempered growths
The canker's spread is sure, so shall this scheme
Thrive in the jealous Emperor's mind. His thoughts
E'en now that way incline.

FAUSTA.

There is no time.

VILERNUS.

Crispus shall not approach the Emperor
Until to-morrow's noon.   To Constantine
This very night——

FAUSTA.

Be it your work, not mine.

VILERNUS.

Harken attentively.   You shall, I say,
This very night fly to the Emperor's tent,
As if affrighted by the noisy guards
Around the royal tents.   There, with the wiles
To woman known, gasp forth in broken words,
"Oh, save your life, my Lord!"—"The Prince!
    The Prince!"
He will connect the words.   The guards themselves
Shall give occasion to this seeming fear
By din and drunkenness.

FAUSTA.

If by these words
Aught happens harmful to the Prince's life,
Be yours the fault, not mine.   [*Exit* FAUSTA.

B

VILERNUS.

Incredible !
To do the deed and dally with the name.
Empress ! unfit for rule.   Woman ! who would
Heaven conciliate and work with hell.
Aurelius waits : there is no time to lose.
        [*Claps his hands, and* AURELIUS *enters.*

AURELIUS.

What shall be done ?

VILERNUS.

Nought left undone, by which we can retrieve
Our hopes so shattered, unexpectedly.
Pronounce the names of Crispus' officers,
Of those in whom he most confides.   We must
This coming night acquaint the Emperor
With some conspiracy against his throne,
The which conspiracy we now shall hatch.
Our brains, Aurelius ! our brains ! our brains !
No man has friends, but some will play him false ;
No man has power, but he offends some friend.
Are there none such among the Prince's friends ?

AURELIUS.

Among Prince Crispus' friends? Yes. He may do.
There is one man—still, I think, officer
Among the Prince's household retinue—
Might aid our work.

VILERNUS.

       The German, Attalus?
Most like, he's deep in debt, and, on that score,
Has been refused promotion by the Prince.

AURELIUS.

The Prince's gold has twice discharged those debts:
He owes some gratitude.

VILERNUS.

       It has been paid.
And gratitude, once paid, is ever paid.
Each act in friendship lives alone, the old
Obliterated quite by later deeds,
And cancelled is his former gratitude
By the withheld promotion. He will do.
I know full well his facile character.
I'll see him presently, he shall confess,

As if in fear of death, some fancied plot,
Half hatched in German forests, ere this war
Recalled too soon the legions from the Rhine.

AURELIUS.

But will the Emperor credit these reports?
For he is most astute.

VILERNUS.

                    The most astute
Distrust and passion blind; the pile's been built
In his ripe mind, we but apply the spark.
Crispus is Spartan in his discipline.
He wars, he says, for peace, and has ere now,
On grounds of discipline, captains dismissed
Caught in the act of lawless pillaging.
Obtain such witnesses.

AURELIUS.

                    They shall be found.

VILERNUS.

Further, act thus.   Whisper in open ears.
The Emperor will be pleased by flattery
Of that successful warrior, his son.

AURELIUS.

It shall be done.

VILERNUS.

                Provide such pregnant hints
As will enable Nasso to expand
Into an epic this day's victory ;
Let him present it to the Emperor.
See that the drinking of the guards be deep,
And that the various officers, their praise
Full of the Prince's deeds, do not omit
His civic virtues also to commend.
Do what I bid.

AURELIUS.

        Sir, I attend your words.

VILERNUS.

See that the fool presents his folly, then,
The officers their praise.   Persuade in camp
That music, incense to their Emperor,
Are clamour and foul breath.   Be diligent.
                  [*Exit* AURELIUS.
I'll to the Emperor, and I'll succeed ;
Extremes in nature wed, are vast in force ;

And torch of hell to set the world aglow ;
The fire of intellect, without the dews
Of conscience, pity, virtue, or remorse !

SCENE II.

Hall in Palace.   Guards drawn up.

Enter AURELIUS.

AURELIUS.

What weighty news is this your silence holds ?
Wherefore so mute ?

1*st* GUARD.

We fear the Emperor.

AURELIUS.

And so assume such visages as befit
Disgrace, surrender, lack of corn and wine,
Retreat from foes, and death of general ?
Mine honest friends, on such a night as this,
When all the camp's astir with gaiety,

Rather rejoice, drink to the jolly Prince ;
Let care be banished hence, shout for the Prince.
                              [*They shout.*
Again, once more—Long live our merry Prince !
What waits outside will aid you to carouse,
To drink his health, long life, prosperity.

1*st* GUARD.

Most gallant Prince !

2*d* GUARD.

                    Most liberal Emperor !

AURELIUS.

Most liberal Emperor ! [*Aside.*] In this full bowl
Shall lie destruction to Prince Paradox !
                              [*Exit* AURELIUS.

1*st* GUARD.

Here comes the Emperor !

2*d* GUARD.

                    No, but the Lords.
          [*Enter* VILERNUS *and* COURTIERS.

VILERNUS.

Our gracious Emperor's presence will enrich
This court immediately.   He is rejoiced,
And deems this lengthy siege must terminate,
Now the so strict encompassed town has lost
That arm that chiefly nourished; nor is't strange,
That he who has the impediment removed,
Should find high favour in the Emperor's eyes.

1*st* COURTIER.

Such bias is most natural.

2*d* COURTIER.

                        Indeed,
It would be most unnatural otherwise.

VILERNUS.

Then let who love him pray perfidious friends,
With but their own base interests at heart,
May not seek honours only at the cost
Of flattering phrases.

1*st* COURTIER.

                 Heaven forfend !

2d COURTIER.

Amen !

Are his affections, then, indeed so warm ?
Is he in such a humour ?

VILERNUS.

Such, indeed.

'Tis but in reason to suppose him pleased ;
Licinius, his rival, is no babe
To meet in war ; thrice have his banners fallen,
And thrice, with speed hardly imaginable,
Has he again collected gold and men—
The Emperor comes himself.

[*Enter* CONSTANTINE.

1st COURTIER.

All hail ! All hail !

2d COURTIER.

Most potent Ruler of the Roman State,
Health, peace, long rule, prosperity. All hail !

CONSTANTINE.

My Lords and gentlemen, our heartfelt thanks.

Heaven has blessed our arms, our admirals
Report dispersal of the routed foe,
And open passage for our needed corn.

1*st* COURTIER.

Let me be first, on this auspicious day,
In my congratulations to the sire
Of the most gallant Prince.   In every tent
His name exhilarates age, and holds to youth
A bright exemplar.

2*d* COURTIER.

                        Princes, Emperor,
Hostages in your camp, esteem themselves
Fortunate in their knowledge of your son,
Whose warlike fame no leader has attained
So soon in youth ; while all, tho' praising him,
Agree to censure the rash hardiness,
Its sole excuse his youth, by which a life
So needful for the State was hazarded.
Prince Crispus to the war-god's very throne,
Has at a bound attained.

CONSTANTINE.

                        The war-god's throne !

LACANTIUS.

In praise of son, men praise the father too.
Most gracious Emperor, the Prince received
Those general orders, which were carried out.
Men rather praise the leader's deep designs,
Than those who execute his purposes.

VILERNUS.

The Prince to widest latitude lays claim.

LACANTIUS.

'Tis false.   His words are garbled by his foes ;
Such speech he never tongued, for he is one
Of those in whom praise modesty begets.

CONSTANTINE [*to* VILERNUS].

Have you had speech with him since his return ?

VILERNUS.

Had speech with him ?   There was too thick a
    ring
Of his most bold and forward officers.
From the tumultuous shouts with which the men
Greeted his least remark, a kingdom's sack
Might have been in debate.

CONSTANTINE.

Did they so shout?
As for the Prince himself, we are amazed,
We are astonished at such arrogance;
My Lords, you strangely overestimate
The Prince's personal share in this success.
Had we not deemed accomplishment not hard
Of our designs, in person we had led
Our naval force; tho' triumph on the seas
Merits, in any case, the lesser praise,
Where chance so much determines the event.

1st COURTIER.

Men are at mercy of the waves and winds,
And I, for my part, meant no more than that
Your Highness's influence e'en extends its weight
To those who war on your behalf.

2d COURTIER.

Nor have
Men even temporarily forgot
That the Licinian force by land and sea,
Has been for months amazed and terrified
By the unceasing progress of the siege,
The battering-rams and moving towers that top

Byzantium's crumbling walls.   Again, the Prince
Throughout the German wars has had command
Of legions trained to service by his sire.

LACANTIUS.

They are not friends to Crispus, who speak aught
Of him but such as best beseems a son.

VILERNUS.

But friends to Constantine.

CONSTANTINE.

              Vilernus, thanks.
We doubt not of your loyalty ; but hark !
What shouting's this, contagious in its growth,
That spreads throughout the camp ?

VILERNUS.

              'Tis he, the Prince,
Who through the camp doubtless perambulates.

LACANTIUS.

The Prince, since landing, wearied from the war,
Writes in his tent.
            [*Shouting and rioting heard.*

CONSTANTINE.

By heavens ! our very guards ;
Instantly bid him here—their officer,

[*Enter* OFFICER.

Is there an insurrection in the camp ?
Is there a sally from Byzantium ?
Why this unmannerly din, so near our throne ?
Bid instant silence, or depart from court.

[*Exit* OFFICER.

How now ?   Have interruptions here no end ?

[*Enter* FAUSTA *and* LADIES.

Who are these now ?   Fausta !   Our Empress
here !

FAUSTA.

O Constantine, arm ! arm !

CONSTANTINE [*starting up*].

Arm ! arm ! 'gainst whom ?

FAUSTA.

'Gainst whom ?   Oh, I am wrong ; let me retire.
I was informed, most falsely, that the——

CONSTANTINE.

Ha!

Vilernus, stay with us; the rest, retire.
            [*Exeunt* LADIES *and* COURTIERS.
Fausta, your fears explain.

FAUSTA.

My fears, my Lord,

Are mine alone.

CONSTANTINE.

You make them also ours

By this most strange demeanour. Waste no
    words.
Confess of whom you spake, and why such fear.

FAUSTA.

O Constantine! if by my random words
I should 'twixt sire and son—oh pardon me—
Forget my speech, 'twas but a part I played,
My tears were false, my terror merely feigned.
I'll swear it by the gods.

CONSTANTINE.

Enough! enough!

Speak, Empress, instantly, and to the point.

FAUSTA.

My Lord, we dare no longer hesitate ;
This night, as to the men's uproarious din
We hearkened most perplex't, even then a cry
Was heard, " He comes, fly from Prince Crispus,
    fly,
They have proclaimed him Emperor in the camp."
But I will swear 'tis false.

CONSTANTINE.

              Fausta, 'tis true.

FAUSTA.

Traitors have spread it to Prince Crispus' harm.
Constantine, be not rash.

CONSTANTINE.

             Woman, away !
                [*Exit* FAUSTA.
By heavens ! when such reports can live and
    breed,
There must exist some damnèd facts beneath.
After three sequent victories o'er the foe,
Was I once lauded thus ?—If men could stand
Crescent rather than full, in morn than noon—

Were ballads made for me? Yet now their lungs
Men burst in his behalf, "for Constantine
Has routed oft most mighty foes on land,
But Crispus on the dreaded sea." Away!
For he must know all this. What would he more
Than seize the crown itself? Vilernus? Ho!
Vilernus, you should love me.

VILERNUS.

Should, indeed.
You have advanced me from most humble rank—
And men promoted love their furtherers—
To be the councillor of a mighty throne.

CONSTANTINE.

No more. Confess your thoughts about the
Prince.

VILERNUS.

I have no thoughts.

CONSTANTINE.

You have no thoughts? Then speak.
Do you know aught?

C

VILERNUS.

   The German, Attalus—
Not among those for whom the Prince desires
Honours and gold—knows all I know, and more.
He is desirous that he may confide
To thine own ears the fell conspiracy.

CONSTANTINE.

Conspiracy !   What ! has it come to that ?
Oh traitorous Prince !

VILERNUS.

   It is most horrible.

CONSTANTINE.

Most horrible.   There shall be justice done,
Tho' it should hurl us from our very throne.
Proof we demand—proof undeniable.
Where are the men who know of this dark
  scheme ?

VILERNUS.

The men await.   One is an officer,
One of Prince Crispus' officers, who heard
The revelation of the deep-laid plot.
Another, captured by the enemy,

In apprehension and by accident
Saw his despatches opened, and therein,
To his amazement, heard the devilish plans.

CONSTANTINE.

These papers were preserved?

VILERNUS.

Sire, they were not.
This man, with one companion—also here,
And also cognisant of the affair—
Escaped their captor's hands, but in the woods
Hardly evaded death, and lost their all.

CONSTANTINE.

We'll hear their tales.

VILERNUS.

Aurelius? Ho!
[*Enter* AURELIUS.

AURELIUS.

My Lord.

VILERNUS.

Bring forth the officers, the Emperor
Will hear them speak.

AURELIUS.

His will shall be obeyed.

CONSTANTINE.

'Tis most unnatural! most horrible!

[*Enter* ATTALUS.

ATTALUS.

Long live the Emperor!

CONSTANTINE.

Speak, Attalus,
Your still unpublished tale.   Speak only truth.
We shall be just, but also merciful.

ATTALUS.

Some days, great Emperor, now have passed away
Since our return from the far German wars;
Blame not my loyalty, nor yet my zeal,
For this delay; sooner I could not speak.
Either the Prince suspects me, or by chance
He has detained me ever by his side.

CONSTANTINE.

Spare us a long preamble, and proceed.

ATTALUS.

Then to proceed.   While our victorious arms
Pursued the flying peoples of the south,
Shortly before the Prince received the news
That peace was ended with Licinius,
To me, 'mong others, had been offered gifts
And future honours if I would take oath
To him as Emperor, and would conspire
Against your royal throne and life.   In this—
For many stipulated for your life,
While he urged strongly that that life would be
The rallying point of scattered partisans,
And therefore counselled death—in this, I say,
He was not followed, save by personal friends.

CONSTANTINE.

The intention's everything; but speak, proceed.
Is there no more?

ATTALUS.

                    Just ere the tents were struck,
Once more were gathered these conspirators.
I was not there, having been sent to treat
Concerning peace with Hercannus.

CONSTANTINE.

But yet?

ATTALUS.

It is believed, for rumours have got wind,
That till the.termination of the war
Now waged against Licinius, their force
Will be directed 'gainst the common foe.

CONSTANTINE.

The chick is still in shell, ere it be hatched
We'll break the egg.   We owe you present thanks,
And shall find future means to pay our debt.
                              [*Exit* ATTALUS.
Alas!
No humble home has nourished son so vile.
When empire tempts, worthless are nature's ties!
Oh heavens! but we will hear the whole—
While sorrow dulls the sense, let us hear all.
We wait the other's speech, let him come forth.

VILERNUS.

He waits, my Lord, to know your royal commands.
                              [*Exit* VILERNUS.

CONSTANTINE.

Is there no truth in dreams? no warnings vague
From senses subtler than are named? My dreams
Have proved premonitors to this event.
My senses find an answer to their fears—
Cloudy, obscure, but not less genuine
In the revealing of this treachery.
But we have heard the worst, for what remains
Can but corroborate.

      [Enter VILERNUS *and* DECIUS.

DECIUS.

   Our greetings, Sire.

CONSTANTINE.

No more? Speak! speak!

DECIUS.

      I only can narrate
How, sent with news to young Procopius,
I with three others in an ambuscade
Was captured and borne off. Our captors found
No meaning in our written Roman tongue,
Therefore, on pain of death, bade one translate.
That reader was myself, and from these sheets

I read—the others listening—how the Prince
Bade young Procopius sound his officers,
And let him know those who would aid the scheme
For murder of the Emperor.

CONSTANTINE.

No more,
But do not leave the precincts of the court.

[*Exit* DECIUS.

We must be swift, Vilernus.

VILERNUS.

Cautious, too.
A nature such as this may well be feared.
Deliberate in conception, swift in act,
The armies love the Prince.   His father's gift
He has inherited of gaining friends.
They—do not doubt it—will his bidding do,
E'en to the uttermost.   His officers
Love him for youth and promises ; for men
Will promise provinces in search of power.
He has been undefeated in his wars.
Now, therefore, if this seems advisable,
Make proclamation of reward to all,
Of safety, honour, and a private ear

To all who, knowing treason, shall confess,
Whate'er the plotter's birth, rank, circumstance.
As to the treacherous Prince, let his high place
Be filled by Fausta's son Constantius.
Arrest the Prince, disband his dangerous troops.

CONSTANTINE.

'Tis good.

VILERNUS.

　　　　The names of those shall be obtained
In whom most trust is placed.

CONSTANTINE.

　　　　　　　And he himself—
Let him be guarded a close prisoner.
To-morrow shall expose his villainy.
　　　　　　　[*Exit* CONSTANTINE.

VILERNUS.

So my plans thrive, Crispus shall meet his fate,
Constantius shall rule, and I in him!

SCENE III.

Tent of CRISPUS.

CRISPUS.

One step the more to our ambition's goal—
The guidance of the world—ambition's goal ?
Ambition has no goal ! our younger wish
Already fades.   The warrior's fame alone,
However great, now seems not great compared
With triumphs won by law, by peace, by thought.
Fame's trumpet drowns, not stills detraction's voice.
Tho' we have enemies—what man has not ?—
Successful action spreads so wide a net,
Few will remain who dare to bar our path.
All friends will advocate our right to grasp
The eastern sceptre from Licinius won.
Metus !

[*Enter* METUS.

METUS.

My Lord !

CRISPUS.

Do messengers await ?

METUS.

They do, my Lord.

CRISPUS.

Let them deliver, then,
This to our Master of the Horse, and these
To our ex-colleagues, Polus, Ammonus.
As to the prisoners, let them await.
We shall adjust the ransoms to be paid.
Let it be known at noon we shall attend
The Emperor at court.   Let Cyrus hear
His presence is desired.   These rolls despatch
To those addressed.

[*Exit* METUS ; *enter* CYRUS.

CYRUS.

The gods abide with you !

CRISPUS.

And with our friends.   See that the bay be cleared
Of wreckage, hazardous to peaceful trade.
Attend the sailors' wants, replant with men
The gaps hewn in our ranks by wounds and death.
The renovation and replenishment
Must be considered of the damaged fleet.

CYRUS.

Immediately, my Lord.

CRISPUS.

And Cyrus, hark !
Be not too strict with our poor mariners.
Wink at their follies.   Those who toil on seas
Obtain their postponed merriment on shore,
Therefore be not too strict.

     [*Exit* CYRUS ; *enter* PROCOPIUS.
     Welcome at last !

PROCOPIUS.

Too late, my Crispus.   Our tired legions have
This hour arrived, to find your battle's fame
Fresh on the soldiers' tongues. Oh, had we marched
But three days earlier, we should have warred,
As oft before, together side by side !
Do you remember in the dawn of youth—
When boyish friendship first had wedded us—
What's life without a friend ?—how then we
  planned
The current of your fame ?

CRISPUS.

     What has been done,
Comrade, is almost nought.

PROCOPIUS.

I hear him speak
In whom praise has engendered modesty.

CRISPUS.

You have heard, too, when others praise him not,
How then he'll praise himself!

PROCOPIUS.

Your words are true,
Tho' tongued in jest.

[*Enter* ARBACUS *and* DION.

CRISPUS.

Welcome on shore, my friends!

ARBACUS.

Ay, Crispus, heaven be praised! on land again.

[*Enter* METUS.

METUS.

The prisoners attend.

CRISPUS.

Immediately.

[*Exit* METUS.

Now, gentlemen, will any wager me
That not a man to be examined here
Has taken to the wars for woman's sake?
Let them approach.   Our guards remain outside.
We shall the fruit of wisdom pluck from boughs
Of knowledge.

PROCOPIUS.

From the grain of knowledge reap
Harvest of wisdom !

CRISPUS.

Or, a third time tried,
Honey of wisdom from the flowers secrete
Of knowledge !

PROCOPIUS.

A sweet metaphor indeed !

CRISPUS.

Here come the prisoners, they shall fare well.
For from the cup of victory we can spare
The spice of gold.

[*Enter* PRISONERS.

My Lords, fortune has proved
Adverse to you in war.   Search now your hearts.

Nothing conceal, reserve, or amplify,
But let us know the causes which induced
Enlistment in Licinius' armament.
Your answers, bear in mind, shall ransom you.
Withdraw, save one—singly we answers hear.
Now, sir, you shall speak first, and recollect
Your answer ransoms you.

1st PRISONER.

                Truly, great Prince,
Amelioration of my fortunes first
Led me to war !

CRISPUS.

             Fortunes, unfortunate !
We shall not ransom those on whom the loss
Will personally fall.   No, by the gods !
Without one jot of ransom we have gained
So much already, we should scorn to touch
A coin of private gold ; and now, attend.
Will you adventure fortune under us ?
We marked in war your valorous quality.
Go now redeemed, and let us presently
Your verdict know.
                [*Exit* 1st PRISONER.

You know him, Arbacus,
Had all Licinius' captains stood so firm
Our triumph had been theirs.

[Enter 2*d* PRISONER.
We wait your words.

2*d* PRISONER.

Ambition, Prince, led me to take up arms.
Allow me, Prince, to serve——

CRISPUS.

Ourselves'? Not so.
For such as you seek but for stepping-stones
'Mongst those whom you obey. Go now dismissed,
And in ambition's fruit remember us.

2*d* PRISONER.

Most generous Prince, deep thanks.

[Exit 2*d* PRISONER.

PROCOPIUS.

How stands the case?
Ambition! wealth! No woman's yet been named.

CRISPUS.

Not all have been examined.

[*Enter* 3*d* PRISONER.
You may speak,

Your motives let us know.

3*d* PRISONER.

Prince, I desired

Favour in ladies' eyes.

CRISPUS.

Said I not so?

PROCOPIUS.

You win no wager tho'.

CRISPUS.

Her ransom is—

How shall we estimate her price, my Lords?
But she is young, fair, opulent no doubt,
Two hundred golden pieces is her price.

3*d* PRISONER.

Her ransom, Prince?

D

CRISPUS.

Ay, to be paid by you.

3*d* PRISONER.

I cannot pay.

CRISPUS.

No, but your mistress shall.
Your wealth's well known, 'tis but a moderate
 sum,
Less than would buy her, jewels, diamonds, gauds.
We'll hear no more.

[Exit 3d and enter 4th PRISONER.
Here is the fourth, my Lords.

4*th* PRISONER.

Prince, shall I speak ?   The lady of my heart,
After most solemn promises, for one ‿
More rich deserted me.

CRISPUS.

So you sought death.
The prick of woman's needle hurt so sore ;
You wished for greater pain, you wished for death,

The greatest ill. Procopius, you see
How women fill war's ranks on land and sea.

[Addressing PRISONER.

And as to you, inquiries shall be made
About your wealth and kindred.

[Exit 4th PRISONER.

Now, my friends,

To court, to court! let us to court apace,
To reap the harvest of our dangers past,
For honour, rule, reward, await us there!

SCENE IV.

Hall in the Court of CONSTANTINE.

Enter CRISPUS, PROCOPIUS, ARBACUS, DION,
SOLDIERS, &c.

CRISPUS.

Constantine not yet here?

SOLDIER.

No.

CRISPUS.

He is late.
[*Enter* VILERNUS.

What holds the Emperor ?

VILERNUS.

Business of state.
But Prince, popular, gallant, fortunate——

CRISPUS.

Vilernus, excellent, noble, virtuous !
Would you have men abhor us, that you speak
With such excessive praises ?

VILERNUS.

I, my Lord ?

CRISPUS.

Or ay, my Lord.   Your speech denotes it too.

VILERNUS.

The Emperor desires there should be drawn,
For purpose of reward, a special list
Of your most bold and zealous officers.

CRISPUS.

By word of mouth, we shall acquaint our Sire
Again with those whose worth most calls for
    praise.
Already, in our papers, have been pressed
Their well-earned claims.

VILERNUS.

              Your courtesy I thank,
And shall inform the Emperor of your words.
                  [*Exit* VILERNUS.

PROCOPIUS.

He is your enemy.

CRISPUS.

            I do not know
Of any reason why it should be thus,
Save that in public, when no more than boy,
In childish jest I called him woman once.

PROCOPIUS.

Does not the Emperor trust him in affairs?

CRISPUS.

Not so, not so ! Not in concerns of men.
                    [*Enter the two* ADMIRALS.
Welcome, my gallant colleagues ! May the day
Propitious prove to all. Here is my friend
Fresh from the frontiers come, and here are those
                         [*Enter* LACANTIUS.
Whom you already know. Lacantius,
I have not brought for you that which I hoped—
The legends I had gathered of the gods
Whom the barbarians worship. They were lost
When we were flooded by the melting snows.

LACANTIUS.

Perchance these myths have interested you ?
Not only for your friends, but in themselves.

CRISPUS.

They have. A likeness in unlikeness runs
Through all these nations' legends of the gods.

LACANTIUS.
I comprehend.

CRISPUS.
                    Then you had known before !

Ere they can comprehend another's thought,
Men must themselves have nourished earlier
A similar idea.   Therefore to know
Is to have known before.

LACANTIUS.

Therefore to see
Is to have seen before !

CRISPUS.

'Tis so indeed.
Originality may then be called
Ability to comprehend.   These tales—
Many still haunt my mind—which, taken down,
May yet enrich your volume on the gods.

LACANTIUS.

My present thanks for future benefits !

CRISPUS.

Also we should be honoured by your thoughts
Concerning some rough draughts which have been
      drawn
To supplement, if possible, our laws
Upon imprisonment and slavery.

LACANTIUS.

They blotch and shame our legal character.
Nevertheless, do not attempt too much.
Remember that those whom you serve are served.
Expect no gratitude or even thanks.
The Emperor at last !—

CRISPUS.

          No ; but the maids
Attendant on the Empress.
          [Enter LADIES.
          Ladies fair,
In absence of the Emperor, the Prince
Thanks you for gracing thus his royal court.

1*st* LADY.

Welcome again, brave Prince, for you have won
O'er our kind hearts a gentle victory.

CRISPUS.

Let from my silence be inferred my thanks.
Great feeling : fewest words !

HELENA.

We shall not thus be cheated of our dues.

1st LADY.

From success, flattery.

2d LADY.

From valour, praise.

CRISPUS.

Ladies, how shall I please?

HELENA.

How but by praise!

CRISPUS.

Why, then, your beauty dumbs——

HELENA.

Out with the word!

CRISPUS.

Your beauty dumbs comparison!

HELENA.

Away!

Call you this praise?

CRISPUS.

The highest praise no praise?
Your beauty dumbs comparison! transcends
Most potent eulogy!   Would you have more?

HELENA.

Oh most unpleasing praise, how have you lost
A thousand similes, but each one poor,
By our surpassing charms!

CRISPUS.

I might have sworn
Sea-shells or wet brown sands were dark and
    rough
By your white shoulders, by your whiter arms;
Your eyes a deeper blue than where the waves,
Meeting the rocks, contrast with the white
    surf;
Your tresses, silk unsleeved: the colours won
From mirrored studies of autumnal leaves,
Rippled, as when, o'er the tall reed-beds, strike
Sharp breezes on the waters till then smooth.
I might compare your beauties to the sun,
Inciting every sense by warmth and light!

HELENA.

Now this is good!

CRISPUS.

Our thanks!

HELENA.

Why, for a man;

For men grow dull!

CRISPUS.

Or rather, women sharp.

HELENA.

In truth they do; for men from age to age
Take such as can most easily beguile.
Your woman-weeding has o'ershot its mark;
Choosing but those whose utmost nicety
Can dart the flying arrow of surmise!

CRISPUS.

We polish then their wits?

HELENA.

Till by their lights

The simpler sex are read!

CRISPUS.

　　　　　The simpler sex
Shall be no more deceived by woman's wiles;
Rather these very wiles are indices.
Thus coldness, hauteur, point to love, desire;
Wit to deceit, or something to be hid!

HELENA.

As wild birds save their threatened brood, or nest
By tumbling flight, or simulated hurts?

CRISPUS.

Thus my thoughts ran.

HELENA.

　　　　　Should we not also know,
And, by our knowledge of your knowledge, gain?
You call us birds! we should rise, shy and wild,
Whene'er the loved and dangerous spot was neared.
Our ways would still mislead; but hark! the
　　　drums.

CRISPUS.

The Emperor at length.　Ladies, the space
Beneath the throne is for yourselves reserved.
　　　　　　　　[LADIES *seat themselves.*

LACANTIUS.

The Lady Helena has wit.

CRISPUS.

She has.

LACANTIUS.

And she is beautiful to look upon.

CRISPUS.

Such things are toys—we shall submit to you
The thoughts that touch on slaves and usury.
How far will interference benefit
      [*Enter* CONSTANTINE *and* COURT.
Must be considered deeply. Ha, my Sire !
Let me, great Emperor, pay the homage due
To age, experience, and authority.

CONSTANTINE [*to* HERALD].

Bid silence in our court.

HERALD.

        The Emperor
Silence commands till his royal will be known.

CRISPUS.

'Tis I, Crispus, your son——

CONSTANTINE [*to* HERALD].

Read forth the scroll.

CRISPUS [*aside*].

What ill's foreshadowed in the Emperor's brow ?

HERALD [*reads*].

" Long life to the puissant Constantine !
The great and mighty Conqueror of the world,
Sole ruler of the Roman provinces.
Here is this proclamation first set forth,
Later, shall be thro' every country known
That there is ample reason to conclude
Treason is active 'gainst the Emperor's life——

CRISPUS.

Treason against the life of Constantine !

HERALD.

" Wherefore reward and honour shall be theirs
Who furnish information of this plot ;

And, as before a clement Emperor,
Those who are innocent will be discharged ;
Informants shall be heard concerning all,
However high in office, near in birth,
Or constant in attendance on the throne."

CRISPUS.

Alas ! my Sire. Think on the powers conferred
By this most dangerous edict, how men will
Rather delators of their enemies prove,
Than lights diffuse on this conspiracy,
If such exist.
For who, now that Licinius is crushed,
Who, in the very apex of your powers,
Dares even dream so great iniquity ?

CONSTANTINE.

That you know best.

CRISPUS.
That I know best ?

CONSTANTINE [to HERALD].
Proclaim
Our further will. Proceed !

HERALD.

" Prince Crispus "——

CRISPUS.

Ha !

HERALD.

" Of his misused authority deprived,
Is superseded in his government.
He is divested of all offices,
Nor may he leave the precincts of the court."

[EMPEROR *and* COURT *rise.*

CRISPUS.

Father ! oh hear me speak ; let not that name,
Sire, be invoked in vain.

CONSTANTINE.

Away ! no more.
Unfilial son and treacherous officer,
Ruthless ! ungrateful ! false !

CRISPUS.

By all the gods !——

CONSTANTINE.

We hear no more.   Guards, let the prisoner,

No longer Prince, stay for the present here ;
Your lives on his safe custody depend.
Let him, however, with the deference due
His royal birth, be watched.

   [*Exeunt* CONSTANTINE, LADIES, *and* COURT.

CRISPUS.

The poisèd edifice of life o'erthrown !
Life's balance, lost !

PROCOPIUS.

   My Lord, still hope remains.

CRISPUS.

Not any. None. I know the Emperor.
You may move death as soon as Constantine.
Yet stay, speed to our friends, report our case.
I know the Emperor, his is no mind
Facile and changing. We must make our terms
From equal strength if justice be denied.
Our troops are staunch, though heaven and hell
  combine,
I'll swear to that. Do not delay. Fly ! fly !

     [*Exit* PROCOPIUS.

E

I doubt, I doubt, this is no hasty storm
Hatched by Vilernus and his damned crew.
Heaven deliver me from this worse strait
Than flood or foe.   Hark ! 'tis Procopius.

[*Re-enter* PROCOPIUS *and* METUS.

PROCOPIUS.

Alas ! all hopes are nipped, all ways are blocked,
Our troops have been surrounded, all our friends
Are in restraint.   Even as I passed by,
Like men in dreams, they rendered up their swords.

CRISPUS.

I have at least been spared their simple blood.
And you—do not be seen in speech with me.
You are my friends ?

PROCOPIUS *and* METUS.

We are.

CRISPUS.

My shoulders, then,
Already burdened, do not further task

With ruin of my friends.   Metus, depart;
And you Procopius, too, most earnestly—
I cannot now command—but do beseech,
Nor will true friends my wishes now deny.

METUS.

Let all misfortunes, wombed in luckless stars,
Be mine——

CRISPUS.

      Call not down heaven's registry;
Obey my wishes.   Should my fortunes rise,
No man shall fill your place.   Farewell!

METUS.

          Farewell!
And if I go, 'tis because seeming foe
Has oft proved useful friend.

      [*Exit* METUS.

CRISPUS.

      Procopius!
We have been friends from youth, your certain
    fate,—
For never falls a Prince without his friends
Sharing his fall,—will but harass my mind,
Not benefit my state.

PROCOPIUS.

                    Would you so act?
O Crispus! is this friendliness?
Do you so lightly estimate my worth
As to desire me traitor to myself—
My nobler self?   Oh, do not friendship call
The light companionship of idle hours!
Oh no!   True friendship's by misfortune sealed,
Soldered by ills, cemented by mishaps.

CRISPUS.

You choose as friend one whom the gods must hate.
                    [*Enter* OFFICERS *and* SOLDIERS.
[*To* OFFICER] You seek the Prince?   Here is your
        prisoner.
Oh, heaven has spite of me, for I have drunk
Ambition's ineradicable bliss,
That godlike draught that makes all else on earth
Seem empty, vain, unprofitable.
Who taste the cup of higher happiness,
Poison for aye the wells of lower joy!

ACT SECOND.

SCENE I.

Nicomedia.   Open space near the Palace.
Crispus *and* Procopius *talking.*

CRISPUS.

How tedious the days !

PROCOPIUS.

It is our third
Month now at Nicomedia.

CRISPUS.

Our third !—
Time ! time !   Procopius, the days speed by,
And every moment brings us nearer death
And nothing noble done.   No great name left ;
No kingdom built or knit ; no wisdom tongued ;

No happier people in their father's homes;
Nought done to cancel debts we owe to time.
So short a space to breathe, the very brutes
Outreach our span!
Procopius, one life! but one, but one!
And I? to die and be forgotten—share
With babes and slaves and fools one common
    end,—
My birth unchronicled! my name unknown!
When, by the gods! I could have won such fame,
That poets would have sung my warlike deeds,—
That nations, yet unborn, my memory
Would have revered,—that to the coming times,
Blazoned with heroes and with gods, my name
Had lent deep oaths a deeper weight—
That men had sworn by Crispus as by Jove.
And now—
Oh waste! waste! waste!
If men knew but their best!   Procopius,
You know how I have aimed at excellence,
At balance, wisdom, judgment, self-command.

PROCOPIUS.

Alas, my friend! I know it all, and yet
I can say nought that is not known to you.

He is an earnest friend—Lacantius—
And bids us hope.

CRISPUS.

Hope !   I have hoped all hopes.

PROCOPIUS.

Our liveliest chance is that the Emperor,
By shame, not love compelled, should yet restore
Your former powers.

CRISPUS.

No reason's been alleged.
He will not hear us speak, nor even deign
Petitions oft-repeated to peruse.

PROCOPIUS.

By hints let drop by Lady Helena,
Vilernus, and the Empress, it is said,
Feed the suspicions of the Emperor
With fancied plots against his life and throne.

CRISPUS.

Emperor or Empress, which you like ; but mark !
Who are these men, Procopius, whom the crowd
So throng with reverence and respect ?

PROCOPIUS.

These men ?

They hail Lacantius, he speaks with one ;
Question him, he will know.

[*Enter* LACANTIUS.
Lacantius,

Who are these men ?

CRISPUS.

Their lives and histories ?

LACANTIUS.

Hermits are they, who from the burning sands
To heal the ailing Fausta have come forth.

PROCOPIUS.

The ailing Empress heal ?

CRISPUS.

Their rank and names ?
Tell us their occupations and their lives.

LACANTIUS.

Worship of God, the cure of mankind's ills.

CRISPUS.

What is this man's especial history,
Who glances supercilious on the crowd?

LACANTIUS.

This man is one who has outlived content;
To whom no longer silken canopies,
Long trains of slaves and viands delicate,
Gathered from farthest lands, would bring con-
    tent;
Who found old pleasures poor and palled, and
    loathed
Habits he once had loved, and appetites
At one time grossly gratified.

CRISPUS.
                        And he?
This man whose frame seems fit to bear the
    weight
Of toil and war.

LACANTIUS.

                A noted captain this,
Most happy in his wars.   A courtier too,
Busied in pushing his affairs,—one who
From nought had raised himself to great estate,

Till, lo! fortune, that changes to all men,
Left him at length in shade. His troops in war
Suffered defeat, and he himself, disgraced
And coldly shouldered by his ancient peers,
Embraced his present life.

CRISPUS.

Tell me his name.

LACANTIUS.

Torquatus.

CRISPUS.

This Torquatus?

LACANTIUS.

He himself.

CRISPUS.

The soldier! author! statesman! courtier! wit!
Has he come down to this? I have perused
Not once, but many times, his books. How oft
Are men unlike that which we picture them!
He then has fallen to this?

[*Pointing to another* HERMIT.

And this man blind,
Ragged, and old, yet even now with marks
Of former beauty?

LACANTIUS.

Features fair were his,
And his those benefits which beauty brings,
Till that disease, that pitted so his face,
Robbed him of half his sight.

CRISPUS.

And this man here?

LACANTIUS.

This man is sprung from lowly parentage.
His cottage, by a swollen river's spread—
He being absent then—was borne away,
And in the waves perished his wife and babe.
That is his history.

CRISPUS.

Does it not seem——

PROCOPIUS.

Does it not seem?

CRISPUS.

Why that, Procopius,
That these recruits are mostly wounded men ;
That the god's service, and man's service too,
Is most supplied by sickness, loss, or fall ?

PROCOPIUS.

It does, indeed, seem so.

CRISPUS.

O heavens ! friend,
Where is there occupation to be had
Worthy man's care ?   Can we, by stratagem,
So force slow nature's growth as to attain
A lasting goal ?
Or alter man ? when 'tis impossible
To force the tendrils of a climbing weed
From left to right, from right to left.   For ills,
Not of the body only, but the mind,
Where is there prophylactic to be had ?
Vain the increase of knowledge.   For its growth
Is none's particular gain, and so it is
That vice and virtue thrive on worked soil
As heretofore ; and as in beams the knots

As well as grain take polish, so men's sins
And virtues grow refined, not cease.

LACANTIUS.

But yet——

CRISPUS.

All occupations are but means, oblivion
The end all seek. I know it now. Alas!
Men still pile cares on cares, care to forego,
And get—but to forget!
The soldier, lawyer, statesman, patriot, priest,
Trouble their minds—for rest! and toil—for peace!
To drown their cares, men opiate their minds.
Business, ambition, pleasure—their narcotics!

SCENE II.

Nicomedia.   Colonnade of the Palace.
VILERNUS *alone.*

VILERNUS.

Who say that virtue in itself succeeds?
Virtue, forsooth! the parasite that clings
To foresight, penetration, management;

How should we prosper else.   Constantius
Rules o'er the Asiatic provinces.
Those who have looked to Minervina's son
Cool in disgraceful shade ; while Constantine
The Emperor himself only awaits
Time and pretext for the last act of all.
Aurelius.   Ho !.   [*Enter* AURELIUS.

AURELIUS.

My Lord.

VILERNUS.

                    Is Metus here ?
Let him attend at once, I'll speak with him.
How strange the inconsistencies of man !
This fellow does not hesitate to swear
A thousand perjuries against the Prince,
Yet from imagination cannot raise
A dozen treasonable sentences.   [*Enter* METUS.
Metus, how now ?   In public you have met
The Prince ?
METUS.
                    I have.   Yet in his rashest hours
He still keeps guard over himself and tongue.
How shall we act ?

VILERNUS.

One other perjury.

METUS.

Villain! I wear a sword.

VILERNUS.

Remember, then,
To what you owe the weapon which you boast.
What have you done but sworn a few score oaths?
Raked up, for sale, a few score lies?

METUS.

Base hound!

VILERNUS.

As surely as the Prince still lives, so sure
Is your immediate death, if my commands
Be not obeyed. As Crispus' officer
Are you still known, a favoured officer,—
All such shall perish,—therefore count your life
From his last breath. When he is gone, you live.
Post to his former troops at Binium,
Use gold and promises to fan revolt.
The train has been prepared, you know each step.

Be swift and secret, count your safety sure
Only by Crispus' death.

METUS.

As for the rest?
Our tools.

VILERNUS.

Our tools?   Let them still be our tools.
I see the Prince approach, do not delay.
Begone at once.

METUS.

I have no wish to stay
To see Prince Crispus, or be seen of him.
                    [*Exit* METUS.

VILERNUS.

Our tools indeed ! our tools !   Why should they
        live?
Men float, or cling, by various qualities.
All men have faults, but those who thrive in life
Are those in whom some force or virtue stems

Currents that set towards death.   These officers,
Stupid, ungrateful, false, why should they live?
With not a single star to light their nights,
Why should they live?   I'll set upon their lives,
When they have stung on my behalf, my feet.
                    [*Enter* CRISPUS *and* PROCOPIUS.
Welcome, brave Prince! you too, Procopius;
Welcome our safety's shield, our honour's sword.

CRISPUS.

By order sheathed——

VILERNUS.

                    Lest he should wound—himself?

CRISPUS.

Those, rather, who would draw.

VILERNUS.

                    You are too keen.

CRISPUS.

Lest I should wound, then, do not play with me.

F

VILERNUS.

Wound ! In some private wounds a nation bleeds,
When lesser men usurp the greater's place,
And thrones are ruled by undistinguished youths.

CRISPUS.

By undistinguished youths ! Call you him so,
Whose victories are stamped in German wars ?
On medals, where barbarians fly ? whose fleet,
Of far inferior strength, the Licinian force
Broke in the Straits of Hellespont ?

VILERNUS.

                        These things
Were by Prince Crispus done.

CRISPUS.

                     Why then, indeed,
Doubtless rich honours have been poured on him—
Wealth, titles, the rewards such as are showered
On a victorious leader in strange wars.
Procopius ! Come, we waste this eunuch's time.

VILERNUS.

Farewell, my Lords !
           [*Exit* VILERNUS ; CRISPUS *and* PRO-
           COPIUS *move on.*

CRISPUS.

That fellow knows our ·wrongs.

PROCOPIUS.

Whence they spring, too.

CRISPUS.

He does.
[*Enter* ARBACUS, DECIUS, *and* COURTIERS.

PROCOPIUS.

Good morning, friends.

DECIUS.

Good day to you, my Lords.   Here Nepos comes,
And primed with mirth.

CRISPUS.

What moves the hoary fool ?

DECIUS.

We marked him laughing with Aspasia—

The frailest girl in Nicomedia—
As we passed by these gates.

[*Enter* NEPOS.

NEPOS.

Now by the Gods!

The sweet Aspasia——

PROCOPIUS.

Let the jest sleep.

NEPOS.

Not if it lies with her! But I am dumb—
Are you for court, my Lord?

CRISPUS.

Are we for court?
Have you not heard our safety is so prized,
We are forbid to venture past these gates?

[*Exeunt* COURTIERS.

Men are like books.

PROCOPIUS.

In what?

CRISPUS.
                              Procopius,
In that they open at the part most used.

PROCOPIUS.
'Tis so.

CRISPUS.
      We love ourselves in other men,
Or why this foolish laughter, born of speech
Mouthed by that scurrilous idiot?

PROCOPIUS.
                              Still,
In ancient Nineveh were merry jests,
And scandalous jokes, be sure, in jovial Tyre.

CRISPUS.
There may have been, but does it not disgrace
This baudy talk 'mong men?

PROCOPIUS.
                        Why! As to that
I do not know, but 'tis 'mongst men the form

Of jest, most handy to their tongues, its parts
Are known to every man. Have you not heard
The talk in camp?

CRISPUS.

I was a man, but now—
By heavens! misfortune makes us girls. My
    friend,
Do you remember—but what need to ask—
That glorious day, when from the pinions spread
Of flying storms, some few and large drops fell?
And how the pregnant and the bellied sails
Induced the wavering admirals to yield,
And cry with me, Advance! Such days were
    worth
Ten million years of this damn'd doubtful life!
But, see! What men are these that cross the
    court?
          [PRISONERS *and* SOLDIERS *cross the court.*

PROCOPIUS.

They are those men whom we watched yesterday,
Sentenced for debt.

CRISPUS.

Alas! these cruel laws.
We need not speak of that which might have
    been.
My hands are tied.

PROCOPIUS.

We heard their various pleas.

CRISPUS.

My ears retain their words : " From no misdeeds,
But mere mischance, my father's heritage,
Sown in the spring of prosperous times, was lost."
" By pity I was urged, not once, nor twice,
But many times, to aid an erring son."
A third spoke thus : " Pleasure has flown with
    mine."
With like results.

PROCOPIUS.

I do remember it.

CRISPUS.

How many paths to the one point converge?
In what does fitness lie?　The same result
Oft to the evil and the good befalls.
There is for man no help save that of time.
Centuries later, what will the world reck
Even of great men's greatest deeds?　Our lives
Are ripples that must late or soon grow faint.
Or—If men could but in negation live!
And own for man no great desire or hope,
Content to not admire and not desire.
To dwell in happy carelessness, to rest
In ease of self, secure within these walls
That shut out darkness, shadow, evil times,
All ills of life debarred.
If—if men could but in negation live!
Earth spins through space, day grows, the stars
　　　appear,
The ortive moon in her own season rounds.
I can as soon the seasons change, or still
Tempestuous winds, or smooth the after-heave
Of the deep ocean's restless breast, as man
By man be changed.　And yet—if mortal could—
I would have snatched down heaven for men.

Heaven !—or hell ?
What demon guides this miserable world ?
What fiends these gods of men, and men them-
    selves
Their makers—men—perjured, adulterers,
Liars, and thieves, in nature vices theirs,
And theirs alone.
And yet—
Do not believe me, friend, in these harsh words—
Mine eyes could weep for man's calamities.
Not the true Crispus speaks—There is no pain
Like pity turned to scorn, and present hell
Are the forced gibes that sorrow's tears conceal.
Oh men, my brothers ! would I could do aught !
Toilers for such a scanty pittance here,
And looking with such hopeful certainty
To future's unfulfillable.   With lives
So brief, these pitiable creatures, half and half
Suffering the double pain transition brings,
By aspiration called, and by necessity,
A twofold voice.   Troubled with hopes, and deep
With memory's disease impregnated.
The most thick-skinned, often most miserable,
Yet sneering still at friends' mishaps, with nought
To stave off time or death, made happy oft

By lies, and oftener still made sad by truth.
Their normal growth by others warped, yet still
Careless in act, and by the knowledge cursed
Of right, tho' powerless to apply !
Oh that the lives of men should be no more !
But hark !   Who comes ?

PROCOPIUS.

The Lady Helena.

CRISPUS.

Be still, seem not to notice her, my wits
Are cased in lead.

PROCOPIUS.

She sees, and will be seen.
[*Enter* HELENA *and* LADIES.

HELENA.

May better days await thee, gallant Prince !
The court removes from Nicomedia
To ancient Rome, where there have been prepared
Most splendid welcomes to the twentieth year
Of your royal father's prosperous reign.

Lacantius gives you these [*giving papers*]. I may
    not stay.
Your friends are watched.

CRISPUS.

      And you are one of them?

HELENA.

He who divinely fails, yet not despairs,
Shall not lack friends. But that a maiden's
    tongue   ,
Must not give utterance to her blushing thoughts,
I could say more. But now adieu.
        [*Exeunt* HELENA *and* LADIES.

CRISPUS.
            Adieu!
Is she not true? Is she not beautiful?
By heaven! Procopius, there is hope—
If not what we desire, yet, even yet—
Oh there is something left, some drug to dull
Life's frets and miseries—a woman's love.
Excellence! honour! name!—farewell! farewell!
This virgin's lap shall prove ambition's grave!

SCENE III.

Nicomedia.   A garden near the Palace.

CRISPUS *and* HELENA.

HELENA.

Hearken ! my Prince, they come.

CRISPUS.

                        And we must part ?
Are there no broken days in all the year,
No dull, uncounted moments in our lives,
That these, our very fullest, should be marred ?

HELENA.

Farewell ! farewell !

CRISPUS.

              Most fair indeed, farewell !
                        [*Exit* HELENA.
By the eternal Gods ! O Heaven ! my own !
My life ! my dear ! my love !—
What atmosphere envelops her ?   From her
What subtlest emanation radiates,

That spring should harbour in her breath and
    hair ?
This is love's miracle I swear, that now
I heard the wild birds sing ! the wayside flowers
Bloomed all about our feet — the spring wild
    flowers,
Though now 'tis autumn ! and the singing birds
Sang as, though dusk, when sun and mist contend !
And oh, my girl ! how can I love her so ?
Why should I ?—caring for her gentleness
And maiden kindness, from her face and hands
And glowing breasts, infer these qualities
Of love, health, charity, but that I know—
But that I know
Each hath in her its perfect analogue,
Surely I could not love her as I do,
But that I know she's good—
Goodness and beauty—
What shall I say that's beautiful—of truth ?
And true—of loveliness ? for there's a tie.
Oh, there is nothing true if this is not.
Beauty is virtue's mask, the which she wears
That mankind may adore !
And me, who am so rough and brusque, she loves !
                        [*Enter* PROCOPIUS.

PROCOPIUS.

Crispus, my friend, what means——
      [*Enter* NEPOS, DECIUS, *and* ARBACUS.

CRISPUS.

                Holloa! holloa!
" Now, for the love of heaven, what have we here?
Ha! ha! What are these creatures? men!
Explain their uses to me. This machine
Is for astronomy, ha, ha! and this
For measuring the earth. As how, indeed?
Why, by the lot? "

DECIUS.

        " No faith, sir, by the lump,—
E'en the whole globe at once."

ARBACUS.

           Where are we now?

CRISPUS.

Why, in " The Clouds," of course.

DECIUS.

You plagiarise.

CRISPUS.

Why, then, I'm honest,—am an honest man !

DECIUS.

In this offence ?

CRISPUS.

Ay, to be caught in it !

PROCOPIUS.

How's that ?

CRISPUS.

Why, 'tis your greatest thief escapes !
He who has stolen from a thousand springs,
Whose sins are by their very number hid,
Is termed original. Your honest man,
Filching but once, is by that once condemned !

PROCOPIUS.

And once condemned——

CRISPUS.

Your honest man turns thief.

DECIUS.

Then we are villains all?

CRISPUS.

A villain he,
A villain I, a greater villain I!

PROCOPIUS.

If he be villain granted, then you are
Greater than he, therefore the greater villain!

CRISPUS.

Greater and less. The greater villain I,
Therefore the less!

DECIUS.

Expound this riddle then.

CRISPUS.

My friend, I am the villain added to,
The virtue superposed weighs down the bad.

PROCOPIUS.

Virtue is therefore villain added to ?
It is a paradox.

CRISPUS.

Therefore 'tis false.
A paradox !   Therefore not false in all !

NEPOS.

True and not true, virtue and villain one !
Is the wise Crispus mad ?

CRISPUS.

What ! has the world
Turned poet, then?

DECIUS.

Or woman ?

G

PROCOPIUS.

Which you like,
Which gender you prefer.

DECIUS.

Not neuter, then.

NEPOS.

What? it! Phrase it then thus—no now known
noun!

CRISPUS.

The part innominate, and thereby named!
Whither away? You too, Procopius?

PROCOPIUS.

I shall return, I seek Lacantius.
        [*Exeunt* DECIUS, ARBACUS, NEPOS, *and*
        PROCOPIUS.

CRISPUS

Ha!—
The wine of folly, pressed from grapes of joy!
From god—to brute! Why, what a thing is man!

Man!
A palimpsest, where the most ancient tongue
Of nature may be read, the alphabet
Of time be traced in letters corporal
On savage man, and dimmer still on brute.
Climate, environment, necessity,
Scrawled on this tract, interpolations here
Of sharp invasion, culture dull and dim—
For age is strength in function,—faint veneered.
Away—for what I am, I am.
Man!
But little lower than the angels are,
His head with glory and with honour crowned.
How resonant to noble touch! how dowered
With faculty of abstraction, like a god
In sweeping generality! whose senses stretch,
Finger the stars, and the invisible see!
Man! who has never lost his gains, despite
Metastasis and horrid avatism!
Who, in elastic darkness, still thrusts back
A blacker night!
Who qualifies—
Who can from very pain and grief extract—
Most wonderful of all!—his keenest joy.
Who wrests from iron necessity, free will,

And from a further yesterday builds up
His wider freedom of to-day!
Oh that my life were pitched at this!
Nought now can hurt.   Oh envious death, avaunt!
Dark death, thy claims forego, now that, once
     more,
Thy face I fear!

ACT THIRD.

SCENE I.

Rome.   A room in the Palace.

VILERNUS *and* AURELIUS *talking.*

VILERNUS.

From Rome Binium is ten hours' ride?

AURELIUS.

At speed,
It can be ridden under the time you say.

VILERNUS.

We may expect at any moment, then,
News of an outbreak of the soldiers there.
Prince Crispus' legions still revere his arms.
Nor have his exploits from the soldiers' tongues
Been brushed by later or more glorious deeds.

All things have been prepared—all things fore-
seen.
Through former intimacy with the Prince,
Metus, his friend, has lent authority   ·
To the revolt ; and of the better sort,
Many have joined the standards of the Prince.   ᾿

AURELIUS.

Metus has proved most useful in our work.
Where is Lacantius ?

VILERNUS.

By Fausta held.

AURELIUS.

Lacantius at Nicomedia !
The Empress too, at Nicomedia !
I do not like it——

VILERNUS.

Hush ! the Emperor.
Mark but his wrinkled brow and angry eyes,
The news desired speaks on his countenance.
                    [*Enter* CONSTANTINE, *attended*.

CONSTANTINE.

Ho, guards! The Prince, where is the Prince?

OFFICER.

My Lord,
Prince Crispus now is seated at the feast
In honour given of——

CONSTANTINE.

No more, no more!
Our guards arrest the traitor instantly!
[*Exeunt* OFFICERS *and* SOLDIERS.
My Lords, we read in every countenance
Astonishment and wonder! Hearken all:
At Binium there is open mutiny.
There they salute Crispus as Emperor.
That youth, these seals and papers prove, has lent
Encouragement to the conspirators,
Has been accessory to their stratagems.
My Lords,
Peruse these letters from our officers
Imploring aid and help; and further, these,
Found on arrested tools and emissaries.
Our life, the kingdom's peace demand his death.

1st COURTIER.

In truth, this punishment has been deserved.

2d COURTIER.

Unless these lie, his life is forfeited.

[*Enter* CRISPUS, *guarded.*　·

CRISPUS.

Where lies our fancied crime ?　Crime it must be.
What other accusation could so drag
A Prince, the son of Constantine, from feast
Given in honour of himself?　Our crime ?

CONSTANTINE.

That which in subject is the greatest crime—
Conspiracy against our throne, our life,
Our Empire's peace.

CRISPUS.

　　　　Oh yet, for what might be,
Allow, allow my friends——

CONSTANTINE.

　　　　Away with him !

[*Exit* CRISPUS, *guarded.*

Who are these men who guard our treacherous son?

VILERNUS.

Not to be bribed, and of sufficient force
Are those who guard the prisoner ; not one
But hates him, bears him animosity
For loss of wife, children, or property.

CONSTANTINE.

Let it be done at once, what must be done.

VILERNUS.

Your will shall be obeyed.

CONSTANTINE.

                And now retire,
For we would be alone.   [*Exit* VILERNUS.
                Most evil times !
Where are the joys of empire that outweigh
Such pains as these ? or can obliterate
A father's pangs ?
             [*Enter* LACANTIUS *in haste.*
         How now, Lacantius ?

LACANTIUS.

The Prince ! the Prince ! for lack of ceremony

Let goodwill plead excuse.   Where is the Prince?
Crispus, your first-born son?

CONSTANTINE.

Call him not son;
No longer son of mine, that treacherous youth.

LACANTIUS.

Traitor!   He, Crispus, Minervina's son?
Traitor!   You wrong him thinking it.

CONSTANTINE.

Wrong him?
'Tis I, his father, who am cruelly wronged.

LACANTIUS.

Most cruelly wronged, indeed, but not by him.
Alas! you speak the truth unwittingly.
                              [*Handing him papers.*

CONSTANTINE.

Whence have these papers come?   I know the
        hand,   [*Reading.*
Ha! but 'tis false.

LACANTIUS.

No falsehood this,
You cannot doubt the facts herein set forth ?

CONSTANTINE.

Our doubts are lively still, spite of your words ;
Eddies, moreover, in the stream of proof
But show the general course.   The rioting
Has been exaggerated, still 'tis true
There have been riots in Prince Crispus' name.

LACANTIUS.

Which name has been by enemies misused.
Incredulous still ?   Haste will not wait.
[*Handing papers*] Read this confession from the
      Empress' pen—
Read of her guilt, Prince Crispus' innocence,
How by the eunuch you have been misled.

CONSTANTINE [*reads*].

" For young Constantius' sake, I have betrayed
The guiltless Prince," Vilernus hatched the plot !

Can this be true?   Great heavens! there may be
    time
To countermand our will.
                              [*Enter* GUARD *with scroll.*
[*Opens scroll*]   But what is here?
Too late, Lacantius!
        [CONSTANTINE *throws down the scroll and*
            rushes out.

LACANTIUS.

            I fear the worst—
[*Snatches the scroll and reads*] " Your will has
    been obeyed, the Prince is dead."
Unhappy father!   Then a crime's complete,
The like of which Rome never knew before.
A frightful tragedy has been in act.
What is more sad than virtue overborne?
Than death in hopeful youth? excepting this,
Most sad of all, the knowledge that the deed
Is one not to be remedied or salved.
Alas! my gallant Prince, too late! too late!
A stormy ending to a brilliant morn.

SCENE II.

Rome. Court of CONSTANTINE.

Enter two COURTIERS.

1*st* COURTIER.

The Emperor grieves, as for a kingdom lost.

2*d* COURTIER.

A kingdom lost may be regained, a son
Once slain nought can revive.

1*st* COURTIER.

               Too true, indeed.
I fear we shall, as years roll on, this act
The more repent, for in degenerate hands,
And in these dangerous times, the city's peace
Might soon be marred. Prince Crispus too
Was such a youth as, e'en in humble life,
His qualities ungilded by a crown,
Men would have praised.

2d COURTIER.

           The Emperor has learnt,
Too late, alas ! the Prince's excellence.
This day, 'tis said, urged by the Christian priests,
He will acknowledge to the assembled court
His jealousy and fault.   And, it is said——
But hush !   He comes ! he comes !
        [Enter CONSTANTINE *and* LACANTIUS,
        attended.

CONSTANTINE.

           Alas ! my Lords,
But faintly symbolised our grief, by robes
Of this dark hue.

3d COURTIER.

          Your people deeply mourn
The virtuous Prince, cut off in prime of youth,
And in your grief and sorrow sympathise.

CONSTANTINE.

Our thanks ; but ere our penitence we express,
Let justice be assisted in her path.
[To an OFFICER*]* Bring forth the prisoner and let
    him speak.   *[Exit* OFFICER.

2d OFFICER.

His mouth is closed, and to our questionings
He stands the figure of negation, hands
            [*Enter* VILERNUS, *guarded.*
Behind his back, silent to everything.

CONSTANTINE.

Let torture loose his tongue.

VILERNUS.

                    There is no need.
I fail, therefore have death deserved.   I fail
Through a weak woman's casual malady.
As to Prince Crispus, do not men present
Donations, liberal gifts, to those who aid
To higher state?   Have not I helped your son,
Your greatness aiding me, to endless years
Of unimaginable bliss?   This fate,
At least, the experienced priests who throng the
      court
Profess is his.   For this you shackle me?
It merits pardon rather, rich reward.
I would not boast, but have I not done more?

Have I not taught a mighty Emperor
To know the beauty of humility?
Made him more fit for entrance into life—
The everlasting life beyond the grave?

CONSTANTINE.

Take him away, vengeance at least remains.

VILERNUS.

Not even that, for thus I baffle it!
          [Poisons himself, and is carried out.

CONSTANTINE.

His lands and goods are forfeit to the sons
Of Crispus' officers, so lately slain.
And let his guilty partner share his fate.

LACANTIUS.

Slay not the mother of your sons.

CONSTANTINE.

                   My sons?
Slay, then, the murderer of my son.

LACANTIUS.
Reflect,

For she repents.

CONSTANTINE.

Away with her !

LACANTIUS.
Alas !

Hardened and obdurate still.   Do you repent ?
Believe, be merciful.   What, silent yet ?
Let fasting, penance, and a hermit's life,—
Allow her time to expiate those sins
That make the nation mourn.

CONSTANTINE.

We grant her life.
Citizens ! Romans ! words can but express
Present repentance, while for personal deeds
The actor's life's required, but art outlives
Both words and actor's life, and shall express
The deep-felt penitence of Constantine.
The very circumstances of throned kings,
Provide temptations not to subjects known,
And of misfortunes of those wielding power,

Greatest is this, that none will dare to speak
Unwelcome truthful words of seeming friends.
There are no checks to kings, and sovereign power
Unchecked, unlimited, is fit alone
For the immortal gods, not erring man.
For man, but by restraints of force can live,
His body of the elements compressed.
So with the mind, shut out from other minds,
The conscience of the world exerts no force,
Men's passions, appetites, desires run wild.

3*d* COURTIER.

That which is past is past, of no avail
Are these reproaches now.

CONSTANTINE.

          There are no words
That hurt, alas ! like this one speechless deed.
Yet—for the sin, yet—if intention's aught,
And if the harvest of the sin be weighed,
There may in ours some mitigation lie.
For from the guilt may be subtracted loss
Of reputation, honour, happiness.

LACANTIUS.

Emperor, credit no such belief! Our deeds
Are children born of us, and for his own
Each man responsible, and nature cares
But for result, or if for purpose, then
But purpose as result.   And though men's sins
May seem unpunished in the sinner's lives,
And though ill - health, remorse, cold looks of
    friends,
May not be theirs, yet think not, do not think
A single evil deed bears not its fruit.
The sinner buried, still the sin descends
From sire to son, a poison of the blood.

CONSTANTINE.

Then does repentance nought avail ?

LACANTIUS.

                    Can aught
Avail your son? what can you do for him?
Yet for yourself, repent ! repent ! repent !

CONSTANTINE.

We do repent, and most unfeignedly.
And lest our penitence should be forgot,
Questioned, or doubted in far future years,
Thus to the coming generations is made known
The innocence of the most injured Prince,
And Constantine's most fatal jealousy.

[*Unveils statue of* PRINCE CRISPUS.

PRINTED BY WILLIAM BLACKWOOD AND SONS.